Karen's Treasure

**Other books by
Ann M. Martin**

Leo the Magnificat
Rachel Parker, Kindergarten Show-off
Eleven Kids, One Summer
Ma and Pa Dracula
Yours Turly, Shirley
Ten Kids, No Pets
With You and Without You
Me and Katie (the Pest)
Stage Fright
Inside Out
Bummer Summer

THE BABY-SITTERS CLUB series
THE BABY-SITTERS CLUB mysteries
THE KIDS IN MS. COLMAN'S CLASS series
BABY-SITTERS LITTLE SISTER series
(see inside book covers for a complete listing)

BABY-SITTERS
Little Sister

Karen's Treasure
Ann M. Martin

Illustrations by Susan Tang

A
LITTLE APPLE
PAPERBACK

SCHOLASTIC INC.
New York Toronto London Auckland Sydney

ISBN 0-590-69193-7

12 11 10 9 8 7 6 5 4 3 2 1   7 8 9/9 0 1 2/0

Printed in the U.S.A.   40

First Scholastic printing, May 1997

The author gratefully acknowledges
Jan Carr
for her help
with this book.

A Rainy Afternoon

Rain, rain, go away! Come again some other day!

I looked out the window. Rain was streaming down. Boo and bullfrogs. It was not supposed to rain in the beginning of May. It was supposed to be sunny and bright. Oh, well, I would call Nancy anyway. Nancy is one of my best friends. She lives right next door. She could come over and we could play inside.

Brrrrrng! I called Nancy. Her mom answered the phone.

"Nancy is not home," said Mrs. Dawes. "She is at ballet class."

I knew that Mrs. Dawes must be mistaken. "Nancy does not go to ballet class during the week," I said. "She goes on Saturdays."

"Actually," said Mrs. Dawes, "she goes a few times a week now. Nancy is going to be in a recital. So there are a lot of rehearsals."

A recital! Nancy had not told me about that. If Nancy had to rehearse all the time, then who would I play with?

I hung up the phone and scuffed into the living room.

"Nancy is busy," I told Mommy, "and it is raining outside. I have nothing to do."

"Did you do your homework?" asked Mommy.

"I finished every bit," I said.

"You could play with Andrew," said Mommy.

Andrew is my little brother. He is four going on five.

"All right," I sighed. Andrew was in his

2

room playing with his Legos.

"Here I am," I said. "I have come to play with you."

Andrew put his arms around his Legos. He pulled them close.

"Andrew," I said, "do not be such a Lego hog."

"Well, I am not sure I want to play with you," said Andrew. "You can be very bossy."

"I won't be bossy," I told him.

"Promise?" he asked.

"Promise."

But as soon as Andrew started building, I could not help myself. He was stacking the Legos wrong.

"No," I said. I grabbed some out of his hand. "Stack them like *this*."

"Karen," said Andrew. "You promised you would not be bossy."

"I am not being bossy," I told him. "I am showing you how to do it right."

Andrew grabbed the Legos back. "You think you are boss of the world," he said.

I stomped back downstairs.

"Andrew does not want to play," I told Mommy. (I did not tell her why.)

Mommy was sitting on the couch reading a book. Reading? It was the middle of a weekday afternoon. Why was she just sitting around?

"Why don't you join me?" she suggested.

"Hmmph," I said. I got my book. Usually I love to read. But that afternoon I did not feel much like it. I stared at one page for a long, long time. Bo-ring! I kicked my legs against the chair. *Bang!* I turned the page and stared at the next page. *Bang!*

Mommy looked up from her book. "Don't you want to read?" she asked.

"The story is not very good," I said. "There is not much happening in it. It is too quiet."

"Sometimes it is nice to be quiet," said Mommy.

Bang! I kicked my legs against the chair again.

"Everything is too quiet today," I went on. "This *house* is too quiet."

Mommy laughed. "Maybe you are not used to being back at the little house," she said.

It was true. I was not. I had been back at the little house for only one day. And the little house was quiet — much quieter than the big house. At the big house there are lots of people. There is always something to do. But I did not say that to Mommy.

Maybe you are wondering what I am talking about. Maybe you do not know anything about the big house and the little house. Maybe you do not even know who I am! Well, let me introduce myself. I am Karen Brewer and I am seven years old. I am in second grade at Stoneybrook Academy in Stoneybrook, Connecticut. And I live in two houses.

I will tell you all about them.

Two Houses

I have not always had two houses. When I was little, Andrew and I lived in one big house. We lived with Mommy and Daddy, and we were one family. But Mommy and Daddy started to fight a lot. One night they sat down with Andrew and me. They told us they loved us very much. "But we do not love each other anymore," they said. Then they told us they were getting divorced.

Mommy, Andrew, and I moved to a little house. Daddy stayed at the big house. It is the house he grew up in. After awhile,

Mommy met another man. His name is Seth. He and Mommy got married and he became my stepfather. Seth moved into the little house with us, and so did his pets. He has a dog named Midgie and a cat named Rocky. Andrew and I have little-house pets, too. We have Emily Junior, my pet rat, and Bob, Andrew's hermit crab.

That takes care of all the people and animals at the little house. Now I will tell you about the big house. A *lot* of people live at the big house. That is because Mommy is not the only one who got married again. Daddy got married again, too. He married a woman named Elizabeth, so she is now my stepmother. Elizabeth had four children already, and they are my stepbrothers and stepsister. Their names are Sam and Charlie (those two are really old — they go to high school), Kristy (she is a gigundoly wonderful stepsister), and David Michael (he is my age, but he goes to a different school).

Do you think that is all the people in the big house? No, there are even more. Emily

Michelle is two and a half. Daddy and Elizabeth adopted her from a faraway country called Vietnam. There is also Nannie. Nannie is Elizabeth's mother. She came to help take care of Emily Michelle, but really she takes care of all of us.

We also have plenty of big-house pets. There is Shannon, David Michael's big Bernese mountain dog puppy. There is Boo-Boo, Daddy's fat cat (he can be kind of cranky). And then there are Crystal Light the Second and Goldfishie. (They are Andrew's and my fish.)

Andrew and I switch houses every month. One month we live at the little house, and then the next month we go to the big house. At first this was a little confusing. Every time I switched houses, I forgot things. Now Andrew and I have two of almost everything: one for the big house and one for the little house. We have two sets of clothes, two sets of books, and two sets of toys. I have two bicycles and Andrew has two tricycles. I even have two best friends. Nancy Dawes (the prima ballerina) lives next door to me at the little house, and Hannie Papadakis lives down the street from the big house. Now, that is really lucky.

Because Andrew and I have two of so many things, I made up a special name for us. I call us Andrew Two-Two and Karen Two-Two. (I thought of those names one day after my teacher read a book to my class. The book was called *Jacob Two-Two Meets the Hooded Fang*.)

It is fun to be a two-two. I like having two houses and two families. At least most of the time.

Bang! I kicked my feet once again against the base of the chair. Mommy put down her book and looked at me.

"So, Miss Karen Brewer, is it hard for you to go back and forth every month?" she asked.

"Not at all," I answered. "I am very good at it."

Mommy smiled. "But it is a little quieter here than at the big house, isn't it?" she said. "That is probably why you have to bang your feet and make so much noise."

I grinned at Mommy. "Well," I said, "maybe *sometimes* it is hard."

Kristy's Idea

The next day, when I got home from school, Mommy greeted me at the door.

"Well," she said, "you will be glad to know that it is not going to be so quiet around the house this afternoon."

"Why not?" I asked.

"Kristy is coming to baby-sit."

"Yippee!" I cried. I love it when Kristy baby-sits. She is not only the best stepsister in the world. She is a gigundoly wonderful baby-sitter.

"I am going to be on a committee at An-

11

drew's school," said Mommy. "So I will be gone a lot of afternoons. Kristy will come over whenever I have to go to a meeting."

"Mommy is helping to get money for the school ship," said Andrew.

"For the *scholar*ship," said Mommy. "We want to raise money for children who cannot afford to go to the school."

That sounded like a nice idea. But I did not wait around to hear the details. I ran to call Nancy. I was sure she would want to come over when she heard that Kristy would be baby-sitting.

"Hello, Karen," said Nancy when she answered the phone. "I am sorry, but I cannot talk now. I am on my way to a rehearsal."

"A rehearsal?" I said. "Again?"

Nancy giggled. "Karen," she said, "you are a two-two, right?"

"Right."

"Well, I have to go to rehearsals all the time because I am a *tutu*!"

I did not laugh. I was sick of Nancy and

her rehearsals. "Have fun," I said before I hung up. (I did not mean it.)

Kristy was in the doorway. She had heard my conversation with Nancy.

"Nancy cannot come over?" she asked.

"She is going to be in a ballet recital," I said. "And she has to rehearse almost *every afternoon*."

"Hmm," said Kristy. "I bet you miss her."

"I do," I said sullenly.

Kristy looked at me. "Well, maybe you wish you had something to do every afternoon," she said. "Like Nancy does."

"I do not want to go to ballet class," I said.

"Maybe you wish you had another hobby," said Kristy. "One that you would be interested in."

A hobby. That was a good idea. "What could it be?" I asked.

Kristy sat next to me. Both of us put our chins in our hands. We were thinking hard.

"I have a lot of hobbies already," I said after a moment. "I am very good at knitting."

14

Kristy already knew that. Nannie had taught me how to knit when I was at the big house.

"Do you want to start a knitting project?" asked Kristy.

"No," I said. "I want something more unusual."

"Hmm," said Kristy. "How about gymnastics? You are good at that."

"No," I said. "I would like to do something new. Something I have never tried before."

Kristy and I thought some more. When Mommy came home, I still did not have a hobby.

"Hi, Mommy!" I called when she came in. I bounded up and danced in front of her. "Guess what! I am going to get a new hobby!"

"That is nice," said Mommy. "What is it?"

"We do not know yet. But it is going to be something unusual. Something *new*."

Kristy picked up her knapsack to go home.

"Oh," she said. "Karen, I almost forgot. I brought you a book. It was a book I liked when I was your age."

Kristy handed me the book. *The Mystery of Millersville Mansion.* On the cover was a picture of a girl with a magnifying glass.

Oh, goody! A detective story. Things were really beginning to liven up now. And soon I would get an exciting, new hobby.

Detective Karen

Kristy's detective book was very good. It was all about a house with secret passages. By Saturday morning I had finished reading it. It gave me an idea. Maybe *I* could be a detective. That would be an excellent hobby for me.

Pitter-pat. Pitter-pat. Outside, it was raining. Not again! "April showers bring May flowers." May was supposed to be sunny.

I called Nancy. Once again, she was at a rehearsal. Andrew appeared in the doorway of my room.

"Do you want to play?" I asked. "We could play detective."

"Yes!" he cried.

"I will be the chief," I told him. "And you will be my deputy."

"What do detectives do?" asked Andrew.

"Sometimes they investigate houses," I said. "They find secret passages. Especially when the houses are very old."

"Cool," said Andrew. "Do you think our house has secret passages?"

"I am sure of it," I said. (Really, I had no idea.)

Just then Mommy passed by. She was carrying a stack of laundry.

"Mommy!" I called.

"Can you wait a minute, Karen?" she asked. "I have to put these clothes down."

I ran out to the hallway to follow her. "But I have a *very* important question," I said.

"All right," said Mommy. She stopped in the hall.

18

"How old is our house?" I asked.

"Hmm," said Mommy. She stared into the pile of laundry. "It was built in nineteen twenty, I think."

"Nineteen twenty! That really *is* old." I turned to Andrew. "Deputy," I said, "we are sure to find a secret passage."

I put on an old, floppy hat that Seth had once given me. It seemed like the perfect hat for a detective. Then I got out my magnifying glass. Now I looked just like the girl on the cover of the book.

Andrew and I spent all morning investigating the house. Since I was the chief, I told him what to do.

"First, knock on the walls," I instructed. "If there is a secret passage behind a wall, the wall will sound hollow."

"Really?" Andrew's eyes widened. He did exactly what I told him to do.

When Andrew knocked on the walls in the living room, Midgie ran in. She barked at us.

"Quiet, Midgie," I said. "We cannot listen for secret passages when you are barking so loudly."

Then Andrew knocked on the walls in the kitchen. Seth popped his head into the doorway.

"Hey," he asked, "what is all the noise about?"

"We are detectives," I explained. I was trying hard to be patient. "And I am the chief. But it is very hard to be a detective when everyone keeps interrupting us."

Seth saluted me. "Sorry, Chief," he said.

I pushed the floppy hat farther up on my forehead. So far we had found no secret passages.

"Let's try the dining room next," I said.

"Can you do the knocking?" asked Andrew. "My hand is getting sore."

I sighed. Andrew is only four. It would be much better if I had a real deputy. But detectives must work with what they have.

"Okay," I said. "I will do the knocking now."

The walls of the dining room were covered with wood. The paneling was old, and the wood was filled with knots. *Rap, rap! Rap, rap!* I worked my way across the wall.

"It is good to knock especially hard on the knots," I told Andrew. "Like this." I showed him.

Bang! A chunk of wood fell out of the wall and onto the floor. Now the knot was a hole.

"Cool," said Andrew.

But I knew it was not so cool. I had ruined the paneling in the dining room. When Mommy and Seth found out, I would be in Very Big Trouble.

A Treasure Map

I picked the knot up off the floor. I tried to fit it back into the hole. Hmm. It did not fit exactly.

"Let *me* see," said Andrew.

"*Shhhh,*" I told him. I did not want Mommy or Seth to come in. Not until I had fixed the knot.

Andrew grabbed the magnifying glass out of my pocket.

"Maybe something is inside," he said.

Andrew nudged me out of the way. He

peered through the magnifying glass into the hole.

"Wow!" he said. "There *is* something in here!" He stuck his fingers into the hole. "Something crinkly."

"Let me see." I grabbed the magnifying glass. Sure enough, there was something in the hole. It looked like a piece of paper. It was rolled up like a scroll.

"Can you pull it out?" I asked. Andrew's fingers are smaller than mine. He squeezed them in and grabbed the edge of the paper.

"Careful," I said.

When Andrew had pulled the paper halfway out, he looked up and grinned at me.

"Good work, Deputy," I told him. "I will take over now."

I worked the paper the rest of the way out of the hole. It was old and yellowed. I unrolled it very carefully. You will never guess what it was. It was a treasure map! I could not believe it.

"Mommy!" I called. "Seth! Come quick!"

Mommy and Seth came running. I knew that they would not care about the hole in the paneling now. I had found a treasure map. We were going to be rich.

"It does look like a treasure map," said Mommy. She smoothed the paper with her hands. "It looks as if it is a map of our backyard. That would be the hedge there. And that is a big tree, probably the big oak that you built the treehouse in."

At the top of the map were three clues. They said:

1. 22 paces from RWSORAB KACB OORD.
2. Turn and face ERED MAREST.
3. Walk to the nearest QUERCUS COCCINEA.

"The clues look as if they are in code," Seth said.

"What is that?" asked Andrew. He pointed to the bottom of the map. There was a signature.

" 'Henry Carmody,' " I read carefully. " 'July thirteenth, nineteen thirty-five.' "

Nineteen thirty-five! No wonder the paper was crumbly. This map was practically ancient.

"What do you think, Seth?" asked Mommy. She looked at the signature. "Do you think the handwriting is a child's or an adult's?"

"Hard to tell," said Seth.

I did not care about the signature. I did not care who had written it — a child, an adult, or a baboon. I was looking at the big ink X in the center of the paper. X marks the spot. That was where the treasure would be.

"Come on, Deputy," I said. "Let's dig up our treasure."

"But it is raining," said Andrew.

"Who cares about rain at a time like this?" I asked.

"I do," Andrew answered.

"Karen," said Mommy, "if you want to, you can go outside by yourself. But put on your rain slicker and your boots."

I could not believe that everyone wanted to wait inside. Soon we would find treasure! I stomped to the closet to get my rain slicker. I pulled on my boots and took out an umbrella. (I would need it to protect the map.) Then I got a shovel out of the garage. I headed for the yard and looked at the map.

Hmm. The X on the map was in between the hedge and the tree. It looked about halfway. I paced off the distance and stood on the spot. I took a deep breath and started to dig. Andrew knocked on the window and waved to me. I did not wave back. I had more digging to do. I dug a deep, wide hole.

Around me the rain grew heavier. It dripped off my bangs and spotted my glasses. It leaked into my boots, soaking my socks. I looked at the hole. It was huge, like a crater. Still, I had found no treasure.

Maybe this treasure map was just one big joke.

More Hobbies

The next day was Sunday. Nancy was going to another rehearsal. I called her early in the morning. I knew she would not be at a rehearsal at eight o'clock.

"What are you doing?" I asked.

"I am about to eat breakfast," she said.

"Me, too!" I cried. "I could come over right now. Then we could eat breakfast together."

"But I am still in my pajamas." Nancy giggled.

"So am I," I told her. "And that is even

better. We can have a breakfast pajama party."

I asked Mommy if I could go over to Nancy's in my pj's.

Mommy laughed. "Okay," she said.

So I put on my slippers and my bathrobe and I poured myself a bowl of Krispy Krunchies. (I would add the milk at Nancy's house.) Then I padded across the yards. Nancy answered the door in her nightgown.

"Ta-da!" she said. She jumped in the air and did a spin. She was already practicing her ballet.

Nancy practiced her ballet all during our breakfast party. She showed me the steps she was having trouble with.

"And I am a little afraid of performing in front of so many people," she told me.

"Oh, Nancy," I said. "Do not worry about that one bit."

I could not help her with her ballet steps, but I knew something I *could* help her with.

"I will teach you how to curtsy," I said. "Curtsying is very important. The better

30

you curtsy, the more people will clap."

Soon it was time for Nancy to go to her rehearsal.

"Do not forget," I said as I walked out the door. I took a quick curtsy, to remind her how. Then I headed home. Now it seemed more important than ever for me to have a new hobby of my own. But what would it be?

I spied the floppy hat sitting on top of my dresser. I certainly did not want to be a detective anymore. My arms still ached from all that shoveling. And my socks had not even dried. I decided to make a list of all the hobbies I could think of. I got out a piece of paper and a pencil.

This was my list:

KNITTING
GYMNASTICS
HORSEBACK RIDING
JUGGLING
WRITING TO A PEN PAL
CARING FOR A PET RAT

READING
WRITING FOR A NEWSPAPER
MAKING MOVIES

Actually, I had done every one of those hobbies. The truth was I was very good at hobbies. But now I needed a new one. Oh, yes. I thought of another hobby. *Ballet*, I wrote. But I did not want to go to ballet class. I would leave that to Nancy.

Later I called Hannie. Maybe her parents could drive her over to the little house and we could play. But Hannie was not home.

"Her father took her to the store," said her mother. "She wanted to pick up a stamp-collecting kit."

Stamp collecting! Now there was something I had not thought of. I wrote that down on my list. I did not think I wanted to collect stamps. But maybe I could collect something else. Hmm, I thought. What could it be? I already had a sticker collection and a seashell collection.

I asked Mommy if she could help me think of a hobby.

"Gardening is a hobby," she said. "And I am about to go out and plant some flowers. Why don't you help me?"

"Okay," I said.

I helped Mommy rake the garden and plant some seeds. Gardening was fun, but I did not think it was the hobby I was looking for.

"Karen!" Seth called me. He was working in the kitchen. "I am making a casserole for dinner," he said. "Would you like to grate the cheese?"

Cooking is a hobby, I thought. I would write that on my list, too. But I have done lots of cooking. I took down the grater and picked up a big hunk of cheese.

I would have to think of a new hobby later.

Solving the Clues

The next day, after school, Kristy came to baby-sit again. She took Andrew and me into the backyard to play freeze tag.

"Watch out for the hole in the yard," I warned her. I pointed to the place where I had dug on Saturday.

"Why is that hole there?" asked Kristy.

"I was following the treasure map," I said. "But it must not be a real treasure map. Because I dug in *exactly* the right spot and there was not one bit of treasure."

"What treasure map?" asked Kristy.

"Here," I said. "Let me show you."

I got the map and unrolled it for Kristy.

"This is cool," she said. "It is like a real-life detective story." She pointed to the clues at the top. "What do these mean?"

"I do not know." I shrugged. "They look like clues. But they must be in code."

"Let's figure them out," said Kristy. "Andrew, go get us a pad of paper, please. And Karen, you get us three pencils. We will all sit at the kitchen table and work out the clues."

At the kitchen table? Boo and bullfrogs. I did not want to sit inside and figure out clues. I wanted to run around outside.

Andrew brought Kristy a pad of paper. She tore off one page for each of us.

"Hmm," she said, looking at the clues. "They look like word jumbles, don't they? Maybe if we unscramble the letters, we will figure out the clues."

Kristy handed me a sharpened pencil. She gave one to Andrew, too. Of course, Andrew could not *really* unscramble the letters. He

does not know how to read well enough. Andrew wrote an A on his paper.

"A for Andrew," he said.

"Good work," said Kristy.

Kristy and I set to work on the first clue:

1. 22 paces from RWSORAB KACB OORD.

Hmm. The first word had an awful lot of letters. I tried to unscramble them. "WAR-SORB," I wrote. "BORRSAW," I wrote. "ROWSBAR," I said out loud. "Well, that is *almost* a word."

I looked over at Kristy. She was busy writing.

"The last word is 'door,' " she said crisply. I looked at her paper. She was right. OORD equaled DOOR.

"You are a very fast unscrambler," I said.

"That is because I started with a small, easy word," she said. "You are tackling the hardest one."

I went back to my paper. Before I could

even get started again, Kristy said, "The second word is 'back.'"

Well, my goodness. She was right again. KACB equaled BACK.

"So far," Kristy said, "clue number one reads: 'Twenty-two paces from RWSORAB back door.'" (She pronounced RWSORAB like "rewsorab.")

I would certainly have to concentrate very hard to work as fast as Kristy. I looked at the letters I was working on. I wrote them down in another order.

"'Barrows,'" I said. "That is almost a word, too. Like wheelbarrows."

"Hmm," said Kristy. "Barrows. Barrow. It is also a last name. I think you solved it, Karen. If you are right, the clue now reads, 'Twenty-two paces from Barrows' back door.'"

I tossed my pencil in the air. Hurrah! We had figured out the first word jumble.

"But what does the clue *mean*?" I asked. "I do not know anyone named Barrow."

"Maybe someone with that name lived

here a long time ago," said Kristy. "Let's go on to the second jumble."

We looked at the next clue:

2. Turn and face ERED MAREST.

I grabbed my pencil. "I will take the shorter word this time," I told Kristy. "You take the longer one."

"Okay," she said.

The first word was easy. I figured it out right away. "It could be either one of two words," I reported. "It could be 'reed' or it could be 'deer.'"

"And the second word could be 'master' or 'tamers,'" Kristy answered. "Or 'stream.'"

"I bet it's 'stream,'" I said.

Kristy agreed. "That would make sense," she said. "A stream would definitely be something that would be on a map."

We had done it again. We had figured out the second clue. "Turn and face reed stream," it read. Or, "Turn and face deer stream."

"But what is Deer Stream?" I asked.

Kristy shrugged. "I do not know. Let's go on to the last clue." We looked at it:

3. Walk to the nearest QUERCUS COCCINEA.

I took the first word and Kristy took the second. We worked and worked on those two jumbles. And what did we come up with? Only a long list of more jumbles.

"I do not think these letters spell anything that is really a word," I said.

"They have to," Kristy insisted. I chewed on the end of my pencil. The front door swung open.

"Hello," called Mommy. "I am home!"

Andrew ran to Mommy. He waved his paper in her face. "Look!" he cried. "I have unscrambled my name!"

While Kristy and I had been trying to solve our clues, Andrew had been working, too. He had written the letters of his name all across his piece of paper.

ARNDWE   DANERW   EDNARW
NDEWRA   WADNRE   RWANED

At the very bottom, he had written his real name.

"Good work," said Mommy.

Kristy and I looked at each other. Oh, well. I guess Andrew was the only one who had solved all of his jumbles.

The Last Clue

Lucky for me, Kristy was going to sit for us again the next afternoon. And the rest of the week, too. That would give us lots of time to work on our mystery. And we would need every minute. We still had to figure out what the clues meant.

When Kristy arrived, we set right to work. Or at least we tried to. Kristy picked up the map and stared at it.

"Okay," she said. "We do not know what these clues mean. So we should write down everything we are confused about. Then, at least, we will know what it is we have to figure out."

"Good idea," I said.

Kristy made a list of our questions. The list said:

1. What is Barrows' back door?
2. What is Reed or Deer Stream?
3. What is QUERCUS COCCINEA?

"Question number one," said Kristy, reading it over. "We need to figure out what Barrows' back door is. We have already guessed that it is probably the name of some people who lived around here a long time ago."

"But they do not live here now," I said. "So how do we figure out which house was theirs?"

Kristy thought for a moment. "I am sure the town keeps records of who owned the houses," she said. "I think those records would be at the Town Hall. Let's go there and look up the information. At the very least, that will give us a good start."

Kristy wrote the words *Go to Town Hall* after our first question. Then she looked at question number two.

"Hmm," she said. " 'What is Reed or Deer Stream?' Maybe that is the name of a stream that is somewhere near here. I think the library has books about Stoneybrook. We can look at those books. Maybe we will find our answer there."

"Another good idea," I said.

After question number two, Kristy wrote the words *Go to the library*. Then she went on to question number three. This one was harder.

" 'What is QUERCUS COCCINEA?' " she read. "I do not have any ideas yet about this one," she said. "Do you, Karen?"

I rested my chin in my hands and stared at the paper.

"It has to be a jumble," I said. "But I do

not understand why we cannot solve it."

"Well," said Kristy, "solve it we will! I am not going to leave here today until we figure it out."

Kristy sounded as if she meant business. She poised her pencil in the air. "On your mark, get set, go!" she said.

And so we set to work. (This time Andrew played with his Legos on the floor beside us.) Still, when Mommy got home from Andrew's school, we had not solved the jumble. Charlie walked into the kitchen behind Mommy. He had come to pick up Kristy and drive her home.

"How is it going, guys?" he asked.

"Terrible!" I cried. "Kristy and I cannot solve this word jumble. We have worked on it a long time. In fact, we have worked way *too* long. I think this jumble is a trick. I do not think there is an answer to it at all."

"Let me see it," Charlie asked.

Kristy handed Charlie the treasure map. She pointed to clue number three.

"'QUERCUS COCCINEA,'" he read. "That does not look like a word jumble. That looks like Latin to me."

"Latin?" said Kristy. She peered over his shoulder at the map.

"Yes," Charlie answered. "We learned about this in biology. Flowers and plants and trees all have Latin names that are their *scientific* names. Maybe this is the name of a plant or a tree."

Mommy had come into the kitchen. She heard what Charlie said. "I have a book you can look in," she said. "It is a book about trees."

"Great!" I exclaimed.

Mommy gave me a Look. I knew I was supposed to use my indoor voice, but I was very excited.

Mommy got the tree book down from a shelf. In the back was an index. It listed all the names of the trees, including the Latin names. I ran my finger down the page. There it was.

"*Quercus coccinea!*" I shouted. (I could not

help it.) "Page sixty-three."

I turned to page 63. The whole page was about *Quercus coccinea*. It turned out that it was a kind of oak tree.

"We have two oaks," said Mommy. "The one by the birdbath — "

"And the one with the tree house," I said.

I had to admit, I was getting excited about the treasure again. This Henry Carmody was a tricky boy. He had made a *very* clever treasure map. I ran upstairs to get my detective hat.

"Detective Karen. On the case again!" I cried.

At the Library

The next day, when Kristy arrived to baby-sit, she called to us from the front door.

"Karen! Andrew!" she cried. "Grab your things. Charlie is waiting in the driveway. He said he will drop us off at the library."

I scrambled to get my things. Then Kristy, Andrew, and I piled into the Junk Bucket. (That is the name of Charlie's car.) As we drove down the street, Charlie pointed to the trees in the yards. "Look," he said. "There is a *Quercus coccinea*. And there is another *Quercus coccinea*."

I giggled. "And there is a *Frupidu lapadu*," I said. I did not really know what a *Frupidu lapadu* was. I just made it up. It sounded like a funny name.

"And there is a *Goopy-goop coochy-coo*," Andrew chimed in.

Charlie pulled into the parking lot of the library.

"Will you need a ride back?" he asked.

"I do not think so," said Kristy. "If we are there when the library closes, Mrs. Kishi can give us a ride home."

Mrs. Kishi is the head librarian. She is also the mother of one of Kristy's closest friends. Sometimes it seems as if Kristy knows everyone in town. That is good for me. It means that everyone in town knows me, too.

"Hello, Mrs. Kishi!" I called out when we walked in the door.

"Shhh!" Mrs. Kishi waved her hands to quiet me.

"Oops!" I clapped my hands over my mouth. "I forgot I was in the library."

Mrs. Kishi smiled. "Are you here to pick up some new books?" she whispered.

"Oh, no," I told her. "We are here to do some *serious research*. We have to find out if there is a stream in Stoneybrook called Deer Stream. Or maybe it would be called Reed Stream. Kristy said we would be able to find some books about Stoneybrook here."

"Indeed you can," said Mrs. Kishi. She led us to the reference section. "Are you looking for a map? One that has details of the land?"

"That sounds perfect," said Kristy.

Mrs. Kishi reached up to a high shelf. She lifted down a large, heavy book. She blew the dust off the top, then brought it to a table for us to look at. Inside were lots of pictures of Stoneybrook as it had looked many years ago. The people in the pictures were wearing funny-looking clothes. In one picture, people were even riding in a horse and buggy.

Toward the back of the book was a photograph of the town. The photograph had been taken from a plane. (Kristy said that was called an aerial photograph.) There were hardly any houses in Stoneybrook back then.

Kristy pointed to a spot on the map. "That looks like the little house, doesn't it?"

Hmm. It was hard to tell. The house she was pointing to looked only like a small roof on the map.

"Yes," Kristy said, "it is the little house. Look." She traced her finger across the photo. "There is Stoneybrook Academy. Up here is the high school. And here is McConnell's Brook." (That is a brook that runs behind our house.)

"Are you sure that is McConnell's Brook?" I asked.

"Sure," said Kristy. "Look. It is labeled." Kristy squinted at the photo. "Oh, my gosh!" she said. "The label says 'Deer Stream.' "

"Let me see," I cried.

"Shhh!" The man at the table next to us turned around and shushed me. I grabbed the book from Kristy. There it was, in black

51

and white. "Deer Stream," it said. Back then, that must have been the name people used for McConnell's Brook. I pictured deer drinking from the stream. Now, there are not many deer in Stoneybrook.

I snapped the book shut. "Mission accomplished," I said.

"Mission accomplished," echoed Andrew.

We had solved the second clue. Tomorrow we would take care of "Barrows' back door." Tomorrow we would go to Town Hall.

10

Stoneybrook Town Hall

Before Kristy arrived on Thursday afternoon, Andrew and I were waiting at the front door.

Andrew pressed his nose against the screen. "I want to play until she comes," he whined.

"No," I said firmly.

"Why not?"

"We have a job to do," I told him. "And deputies do not play during work time."

Charlie's Junk Bucket pulled up in front

of the house. Kristy hopped out.

"Hey, guys!" she said, waving.

I pulled Andrew out the door. "Let's go!" I cried. I did not want to waste any time. "To Town Hall!"

Stoneybrook Town Hall is a short walk from our house. It is a big gray building. Inside, the air smells musty. Kristy pulled open the heavy front door.

"Wow," said Andrew. "This place is spooky. Do ghosts live here?"

In the front hall was an information desk. I marched right up to it.

"Hello," I said. "My name is Karen Brewer and I need some information."

The woman behind the desk smiled. She nodded to the sign in front of her desk. "Then you have come to the right place," she said.

"We need to know if a family named Barrow ever lived in a house on Forest Drive," I said.

"That would be in County Records," said

the woman. "Go right up those stairs and into the third door on the left."

Kristy, Andrew, and I climbed the long flight of wooden stairs. The sound of our footsteps echoed through the building.

The third door on the left was closed. I knocked on it. A man opened the door. He looked pale (probably from being cooped up in such a dark, dusty room all day). The man told us his name was Stuart. He asked if he could help us.

"I certainly hope you can," I said. "Because we are trying to solve our clues. We are looking for a family named Barrow. We think they might have lived on Forest Drive in nineteen thirty-five."

"Barrow?" Stuart repeated. "On Forest Drive? Let me see."

Kristy winked at me. I could tell she thought I was doing a good job.

Stuart opened a file drawer. He riffled through some records. He searched a long time, and then he pulled out a piece of paper. It was old and yellowed.

"Here you are," he said. "Barrow. They did indeed live on Forest Drive in nineteen thirty-five. They held the title to the house another ten years after that."

"Which house?" I asked quickly. "What was their address?"

Kristy shot me a Look.

"What was their address, *please*," I added.

"Number fourteen," said the man.

Number 14. That was Nancy's house!

"Does this mean we will find the treasure?" asked Andrew.

"Treasure?" repeated Stuart.

"Yes," I said importantly. "I am a detective and these are my deputies. We are searching for treasure that was buried in our backyard. Now we are solving the clues."

"I see," said Stuart. "Well, I am glad I could be of help."

"You have been *very* helpful," I said.

I shook Stuart's hand. Then Kristy, Andrew, and I trooped back down the long wooden stairway.

"Thank you!" I waved to the woman at the information desk.

At last we had all the information we would need. Tomorrow we would dig for buried treasure.

Digging for Treasure

On Friday I was very excited. At school I could not keep my mind on my work. I kept thinking of the treasure and all the things I would do with it once we had dug it up.

First I would give a big chunk of money to the scholarship fund for Andrew's school. (Mommy and Seth would be proud of me.) Then I would buy every one of my friends and everyone in both my families a big, big present. And finally I would buy a whole bunch of things for myself. Things I really,

really needed. I would start at the bookstore.

That day, after school, I ran home from the bus stop and waited for Kristy. As soon as she arrived, we took the map outside.

"Deputies," I announced. "This is the moment we have all been waiting for." I read the first clue aloud so we could follow the directions.

" 'Number one,' " I said. " 'Twenty-two paces from Barrows' back door.' "

With that, I walked straight to Barrows' back door. (Actually, I walked to Nancy's back door, but you know what I mean.)

"Okay," I said. I faced our house. "Now we have to walk twenty-two paces."

I started to take a step. Then I stopped. "Giant steps or baby steps?" I asked.

"Hmm," said Kristy. "Medium, I think."

"One, two, three," I counted. "Four, five, six, seven, eight." Andrew called out the numbers along with me. (He got a little mixed up after we passed the number fifteen.) When I had walked twenty-two paces, Kristy read the second clue.

" 'Turn and face Deer Stream,' " she said.

I spun on my heel and turned to face Deer Stream (also known as McConnell's Brook). This was fun. My heart began to beat faster. I could almost feel those gold doubloons spilling through my fingers.

"Now," said Kristy, reading the rest of the directions. " 'Walk to the nearest *Quercus coccinea.*' "

That was a snap. I marched to the nearest oak tree. It was not the one we had built our tree house in. It was the one by the birdbath. It certainly was easy to follow the map now that we had figured out the clues. All of our hard work was about to pay off.

"Okay," said Kristy. She brought the map to me. "The X is halfway between the tree and the hedge. So that is where we will dig."

And dig we did. Before long we had a hole a foot deep and four feet wide. But guess what. We did not find any treasure. None at all. We did find some old tree roots and some wriggly worms, but that is all. My shirt was dirty and sweaty. I plopped myself down at the edge of the big muddy hole. I was beginning to feel very discouraged.

"Hi, everybody!" called Mommy. She poked her head out the back door. Then she saw the hole.

"What in the world happened to the yard?" she asked. She did not look pleased.

Kristy looked at me. "Karen," she asked, "you mean you did not ask if it was okay for us to dig this hole?"

I shrugged. "I did not think of it," I said. "I dug a hole once before. I figured there would be no problem if we did it again."

Mommy looked across the yard and shook her head.

"Well, it certainly is *not* okay," she said crossly. "The yard looks like a war zone. Karen Brewer," she said firmly, "there is to be no more digging in the backyard. And that is that."

I hung my head. "Yes, Mommy," I said.

No more digging in the backyard? Well,

that was okay with me. I was sick of digging for treasure. After all our hard work, there was no treasure after all. Henry Carmody had tricked us before. And now he had tricked us again. I guessed the treasure map was his idea of a joke. A big, fat joke.

Well, I did not think Henry's joke was very funny.

Photos in the Attic

On Saturday I called Nancy. She was busy again, rehearsing for her you-know-what. I did not care, though. Andrew and I could continue with our detective work.

"Come on, Andrew," I said. "We have not finished investigating the house."

"What about the treasure map?" he asked.

"Forget about that," I told him. "We will look for something different now."

Andrew rubbed his hand as if it were still sore. "Do I have to knock on walls again?" he asked.

"No," I said. "Today we will investigate the attic."

"Cool!" said Andrew.

Once again I put on my floppy detective hat. I let Andrew carry the magnifying glass. Then I got a flashlight, and Andrew and I climbed the stairs to the attic.

In the attic were a lot of old things. At the top of the stairs was a couch. I ran my finger across the cushions. They were covered with dust.

"Yuck," said Andrew. He pounded the cushions. Dust billowed up and tickled our noses.

"*Ah-choo!*" Andrew sneezed.

I turned on my flashlight and looked around the room.

"Karen," said Andrew. "We do not need the flashlight. We can just turn on the lights."

"No," I said. "It is important to investigate with a flashlight."

"Why?" asked Andrew.

I sighed. "Andrew," I said, "it is a good

thing that I am chief detective and you are my deputy. I know much more about investigating than you do."

I shined the light in the corners of the room.

"What are we looking for?" asked Andrew.

"We do not know yet," I said. "We will figure it out when we find it."

"Why?" asked Andrew.

"Because," I answered. I shot him a Look. I hoped he would be quiet.

Behind the couch were a lot of boxes.

"First we will investigate these," I said.

One of the boxes was filled with old baby things. Inside were blankets, clothes, and toys.

"Look," cried Andrew. He pulled out a rattle and a teething ring.

"Those were yours," I told him. "You used to play with them when you were little."

"Really?" asked Andrew. He shook the rattle and bit on the ring. "Goo goo ga ga," he said. He fished deeper into the baby box.

I climbed over the rest of the boxes and continued on.

At the back of the attic were eaves. That looked like a good place to find something interesting. Maybe I would find a stack of old letters. Or a skeleton. I shined my flashlight across the wood beams. Something *was* there. A box. It looked as if someone had hidden it there, or at least tucked it away and forgotten it. The box was old. I opened the lid carefully. Inside were photographs. They were black-and-white.

"Deputy," I called. "Bring the magnifying glass!"

Andrew scrambled over to me.

"What is it?" he asked.

"Old pictures," I said. "Some are of people. I wonder who they are."

In one photo a young boy was playing in the yard. He was wearing funny clothes. His pants came just past his knees. They were held up by suspenders.

"That is our yard," said Andrew.

"Maybe," I said. "But that is not our

hedge. And what tree is that? It is not in our yard now."

I turned over the photograph. On the back, something was written in ink. "H. at play," it said. "Nineteen thirty-four."

"H.," I said, thinking. H. might be Henry. Henry Carmody, the boy who had drawn the treasure map!

I looked at the photo again. It *was* our yard. But what was that tree? And why was the hedge on the side of the yard, not the back?

"Eureka!" I cried. "We have solved the puzzle. The hedge is in a different place now. And this big tree must have been cut down. That is the reason the treasure map did not work. The yard is different now."

I clutched the photo and ran down the stairs. "Mommy! Mommy!" I cried. Andrew ran behind me. We would have to call Kristy. There might be treasure after all.

One Last Hole

"Please, can we dig again?" I begged Mommy. "Please, please, *please*?"

I showed her the photo of the yard.

"Hmm," she said. "This is interesting. But Seth and I have talked it over, and we cannot have any more holes in the yard."

"Not only does it look bad," said Seth, "but you could damage something. The water pipes run under the yard. If you keep digging, you could puncture them. Then we would really have a mess on our hands."

"We will be careful," I promised. "Very careful."

Mommy took the photo in her hand and looked at it closely.

"Will you look at that," she said. "The hedge was across the *side* of the yard."

"And the trees were different," I added quickly. "Some of our trees were not even planted yet. And some of their trees have been cut down."

Mommy looked at Seth. Seth looked at Mommy. They both looked at me. I could not help it. I broke into a big, silly grin.

"All right," said Mommy. "We will let you dig one more time."

"Yippee!" I shouted.

"But only *one* hole," Seth added. "This is absolutely the last treasure-digging you will do in our yard."

I ran to the phone to call Kristy.

"You have to come over this instant," I said. I told her everything I had discovered. "Can you come?" I asked. "Can you, please? Right now?"

Kristy hesitated. "I was just about to eat lunch," she said.

"Eat it over here," I begged. "We will have a big lunch after we dig. A big celebration lunch!"

"Okay," said Kristy. "I will be there in twenty minutes."

Just before noon Charlie dropped off Kristy. She and I walked straight to the backyard. This time we took the map and the photo. I walked the twenty-two paces from Barrows' back door. Then I turned to face Deer Stream.

Kristy read off the last of the clues: " 'Walk to the nearest *Quercus coccinea*.' " I walked. But this time I did not go to either of our two oak trees. I walked to an old, weathered stump. According to the photo, it had once been a big, beautiful tree.

"Okay," said Kristy. "Now remember. The X is halfway between this tree stump and the hedge."

"And the hedge was over there." I pointed.

72

Kristy and I walked to the spot where the X would be. She handed me the shovel. I sucked in my breath. Just as I was about to push it into the ground, Andrew burst through the door.

"Can I help?" he asked.

"Sure," I said.

I crossed my fingers and made a wish. I wished for treasure, lots of it. Enough treasure to fill a giant chest.

Treasure!

I wiped my hands on my pants and rested my foot on the blade of the shovel. *Oof!* I shoved it into the ground.

"Now I know why they call it a *shov*-el," I said, giggling.

The digging went slowly. I went first. Then Andrew (actually, Kristy and I helped him). Then Kristy took a turn. The hole got bigger. And deeper. Finally it was about a foot deep. Then it was my turn again. For a moment I wondered if all this digging was worth it. Maybe we were being silly. Maybe there was no treasure and never had been. Maybe all that we had done was fill our yard with holes.

Clink! My shovel hit something. Oh, no. I remembered what Seth had said about the water pipes. What if I made a pipe spring a leak? Seth would really be mad at me then.

Clink! The shovel hit something again.

"It is probably a rock," said Andrew.

"Let me see," said Kristy.

Kristy got down on her hands and knees. She pushed aside the dirt. Something glinted in the sun. Something metal. As she cleared the dirt, we saw a box. Kristy picked up the shovel and pried it out. It was old and rusty. She handed it to me. I shook it. *Rattle, rattle!* Something was inside. It sounded like money. Maybe gold doubloons or pieces of eight. I thought of the speech I would give when I donated money to Andrew's school. I thought of all the books I would buy, the presents I would give my family and friends.

"Treasure!" I cried. I jumped up and down. "We found treasure!"

The box was fastened with an old, bent latch. When I tugged at it, it popped open. Coins flew everywhere, scattering across the grass.

"Yahoo!" I cried. Kristy, Andrew, and I scrambled around, gathering up the coins.

Oh, no. Most of the coins were just pennies. Some were nickels and some were dimes. But there were no quarters, no half dollars, and no silver dollars. And there were certainly no gold doubloons or pieces of eight.

"This is not a treasure," I said. "This is just somebody's old change."

Kristy looked disappointed, too. "Let's add it up," she said.

We put the coins back in the box and counted them out. Andrew tried to help us. He counted each coin as one cent.

"No, Andrew," I said. "This is a *nickel*. It has to count as five, not one. And dimes count as ten." Andrew looked confused.

"You will learn all about it in first grade," I told him. "Let Kristy and me do the counting."

It did not take us long to total up the coins. Two dollars and forty-seven cents. That was all.

"The coins are not even shiny," I said, pouting. "They are old and dull. This is stupid. All that digging for two dollars and forty-seven cents? I cannot buy a stack of new books with this. I cannot even buy *one*."

I thought of the photo I had found in the attic. I pictured the boy in his short pants and suspenders. "H. at play," the photo had read. Henry Carmody was just a boy. A boy in 1935. He must have thought two dollars and forty-seven cents was a lot of money.

Well, it was not a lot of money now. And if anybody thought it was, they had another think coming.

The Coin Shop

"Karen! Andrew! Kristy!" called Seth. "It is time for lunch."

We trooped into the house.

"Hey," Seth said when he saw the box. "It looks like you found treasure!"

"We found something," I said. "But it is not treasure. It is just some old pennies and nickels and dimes. They are not even new or shiny."

"Oh, I'm sorry," said Seth.

Seth had made us sandwiches and soup for lunch. I tossed the metal box with the coins at one end of the kitchen table.

"I do not want anything to eat," I announced. "All those stupid pennies made me lose my appetite."

Seth dished up the soup. It was steamy and smelled very good.

"Are you sure you do not want some?" he asked. He passed me a bowl.

"Maybe just a little," I said. I ate it up quickly.

"So let's see those coins," said Seth. "Let's see the treasure that is not really a treasure."

I opened the metal box and dumped the coins onto the table. Seth picked up the coins one at a time.

"These are old, all right," he said. "Look at this one. The date on it is eighteen sixty-one."

"Wow," said Kristy. "That was the time of the Civil War."

I did not care when it was. A penny was a penny. Seth turned the coin over in his fingers.

"Karen," he said, "I wonder if these coins are worth something. More than their original value."

"What do you mean?" I asked.

"People buy and sell old coins," Seth said. "I think we should take these to a coin shop and have an expert look at them. You might be able to sell the coins for a good price."

Seth took out the telephone book and paged through it.

"You mean there is a store where they buy *money*?" I asked. This was turning out to be exciting after all. "Let's go!"

Seth found an ad for a coin shop and dialed the number. The man at the shop told us to come by.

"Well," Seth said to me when he hung up, "why don't I drive Kristy home? Then you and I could go to the coin shop."

"Can I go, too?" asked Andrew.

"You can stay here with me," said Mommy. "You and I can read stories."

Andrew pouted. He stomped off to get

some books. I was glad I was not four years old anymore.

The coin shop was very interesting. The man who worked there had lots of coins in glass display cases. Some were from other countries. Some were very old. The rarest coin he had was *very* old. It was from ancient Rome.

"This coin passed through a lot of hands," he said. "The hands of people who lived a long time ago."

"Ooh," I said. That made me think about the penny in my box, the one from the time of the Civil War. Maybe a soldier had carried it to battle. Maybe it was a lucky penny and had saved him from getting killed.

The man at the shop asked to see my coins. This time I did not dump them out. I set the metal box on top of the counter and opened the lid.

"Hmm," said the man. He picked up one coin after another. He flipped through a book, looking for information. Then he

wrote down some numbers and made notes on a pad.

"This collection is worth several hundred dollars," he said when he had finished. "I would have to take a closer look to tell you exactly how much. Would you be interested in selling it to me?"

Several hundred dollars! With that much money, I could buy lots of books. And plenty of presents for other people, too.

"What do you think?" asked Seth. "Do you want to sell the coins?"

I looked at the man. I looked at Seth. I thought of Henry Carmody, the boy in the short pants. Maybe he had buried the coins when he was about my age.

"No," I said firmly. "I do not want to sell them."

Henry Carmody

Seth and I got back into the car. I hugged the metal box to me. After all, it was worth a lot of money.

"So," said Seth as he drove off. "You have decided to keep the coins after all."

"Not exactly," I said. "The coins are not really mine to keep."

"Sure they are," said Seth. "You found them, fair and square."

"Well," I said, "I have been thinking. The coins really belong to Henry Carmody. If he was a child in nineteen thirty-five, he might still be alive. And he might want the money."

Seth stopped at a red light. He turned to look at me.

"Karen," he said, "that is a good idea. I am very proud of you for thinking of Henry."

"But how will I find him?" I asked.

"We could look in the phone book," said Seth. "We can do that as soon as we get home. Henry could still live in Stoney-brook."

When we pulled into the driveway, Andrew ran outside to greet us.

"Where is the treasure? Where is the treasure?" he asked. "Did you sell it? Did you get a lot of money?"

"It is right here," I said. "But it is not ours."

"What?" Andrew stopped short.

"It belongs to Henry."

I pushed past Andrew and headed inside. I took out the phone book and turned to the

Cs. Hmm. The names and numbers were very small. They were hard to read.

Seth turned the page to help me. "C-A-R-M-O-D-Y," he said, spelling out the name. He ran his finger down the page.

"Well," he said. "There are no Carmodys listed in this book."

"Then the coins are ours," said Andrew. "Right?"

"Maybe he moved away," said Seth. "This phone book is only for our town and a few of the towns nearby."

I called Kristy and told her what had happened. I told her that I had decided to give the coins to Henry Carmody.

"The only problem is," I said, "we cannot find Henry Carmody in the phone book. We do not know where he lives."

Kristy thought for a moment.

"You will have to do more investigating, Chief," she said.

"But where will I look?"

"On Monday I am coming over to baby-sit," said Kristy. "We will go back to Stoney-brook Town Hall. Stuart can look up the Carmodys the same way he looked up the Barrows."

As she had promised, Kristy took Andrew and me back to Town Hall.

"We are back," I told Stuart. "And we need more help."

Stuart looked up the records on the little house. The Carmodys had once owned it, but they had sold it in 1938.

"Where did they go?" I asked.

"We do not have that information," he told me. "We only know that they sold the house and left."

Now what was I going to do? I had to find Henry and I had no more clues. Maybe Henry needed the money. Maybe he was alone somewhere, without any family to care for him. Maybe he was old and feeble. Maybe he was sick or starving. Kristy put her arm around me as we walked out the door.

"I am sorry this did not work out," she said.

"Sometimes being a detective is *very* frustrating," I said.

"Well," said Kristy, "I have another idea. Maybe Henry still lives in Connecticut, but in a town that is not near ours. The library will have a listing of all the phone numbers in Connecticut. Tomorrow we will go back and search through them."

"Good idea, Deputy!" I said.

I was very lucky. Not every chief has a deputy who is as smart as Kristy.

The Big Phone Call

Kristy's idea was better than good. It was excellent. That is because it worked! On Tuesday afternoon Kristy, Andrew, and I went to the library. Kristy picked out some books for Andrew to look at. Then she asked Mrs. Kishi to help us find the phone listings.

"Can we find them on the computer?" asked Kristy.

Mrs. Kishi checked her catalog.

"Hmm," she said. "There is a CD-ROM with that information. We have ordered

90

it, but it has not come in yet. I am afraid the only way to look is the old-fashioned way."

I frowned. I was not sure what she meant.

"The phone book," said Mrs. Kishi. "We have all of the phone books for Connecticut. If you sit down, I will bring them to you."

Kristy and I found a table. Andrew sat in a chair next to us. He was reading a book called *The Salamander Room,* by Anne Mazer. The book is about a boy who brings home a salamander.

"Can I have a salamander?" Andrew asked.

"Sure," I said. I was not really paying attention.

"When?" asked Andrew.

"Oh, Andrew," I said, "We cannot worry about salamanders now. We have to find Henry Carmody."

Mrs. Kishi brought us a stack of phone books. Then she disappeared and came back with a second stack. Then a third.

I slumped down in my chair. "Help!"

I cried. "We are being buried by phone books."

"Do not worry," Kristy assured me. "It will not take us long to search through them. We have to look up only one name in each book."

We did not find any Carmodys in the first book. Or the second. Or the third. I was beginning to think that Henry Carmody had disappeared. Maybe he had moved someplace far away. Maybe he had moved to China. Or to Paris, France.

Finally we found a Carmody. But it was Lucille Carmody. In the next book, we got luckier. "Carmody, H." it said.

I copied down the number and snapped the book shut.

"Great," I said. "Now we can go home."

"Not yet," said Kristy. "Maybe that is not the right H. Carmody. We need to go through *all* the books. That way we will find all the Carmodys in Connecticut."

Boo and bullfrogs! I wanted to call H. Carmody right away.

"Be patient," said Kristy. "We are almost through."

Hmm. Sometimes I am not very good at being patient.

Finally we worked our way through all the books. We did not find any listings for Henry Carmody. But we did find another "Carmody, H." Maybe one of the two was Henry. There was only one way to find out.

"Back to the house," said Kristy.

As soon as we got home, I ran to the phone.

"Wait a minute," said Kristy. "Before you call, you should think about what you are going to say."

That was simple. "I will ask for Henry Carmody," I said.

"And then what?"

Hmmm. "I will ask him if he ever lived in Stoneybrook, at Twelve Forest Drive. Then I will ask him if he ever buried a box of coins."

Kristy nodded. "Sounds good," she said.

I took a deep breath and dialed.

The first H. Carmody was not Henry. It was a woman named Hannah Lee.

"Do you know of a man named Henry Carmody?" I asked. Maybe Henry was her brother or her father.

"No," she said. "I am sorry. I do not know anyone named Henry."

Boo and bullfrogs. I hung up and dialed the second number. This time a man answered the phone. My heart started pounding.

"May I please speak to Henry?" I asked.

"This is Henry," he said.

I forgot all about staying calm.

"Henry!" I cried. "I am so glad we found you. Kristy and I looked up your name in every Connecticut phone book. I did not know what I would do with the coins if I did not find you."

There was a long pause on the other end of the phone.

"And who is this?" he asked.

Oh. I had not explained a thing about who I was or why I was calling. Oops. I

94

cleared my throat. I would have to start over.

"This is Karen Brewer," I said more calmly. "I live at Twelve Forest Drive, in Stoneybrook. I know from the county records that you used to live here, too. Or at least someone named Henry Carmody did. Was that you?"

"My goodness," said Henry. "Indeed it was. Why, that was a long time ago."

"Yes, it was," I said. "You moved away in nineteen thirty-eight. Anyway, a few weeks ago I found a treasure map stuck inside the wall in the dining room. It had your name on it. Do you remember making a treasure map?"

"A treasure map?" he said. "No. I cannot say I remember anything of the sort."

"It was for coins," I went on. "You buried them in the backyard."

"My goodness," said Henry. "Coins, eh?"

"The coins are worth money now," I told Henry. "And they belong to you."

Henry was very surprised to hear my

news. In fact, he was very surprised to hear from me at all.

"What an adventurous girl you must be," he said.

"That is because I am a detective," I explained.

I told Henry I would ask my parents to call him when they got home. They would be able to get the coins to him. Then it was time to hang up.

"Thank you very much for calling, Karen," said Henry. "I certainly look forward to meeting you."

And I looked forward to meeting Henry. (I wondered if he still wore short pants with suspenders.)

Visiting Henry

On Sunday we drove to Henry's house. The ride was very long. It took a whole hour.

"Karen," said Seth, "I have a good job for you. Your job is to keep all of us entertained while we are in the car."

"Okay," I said. I am very good at keeping people entertained. "I know. We will play a game. The game will be called 'I Wonder What Henry Is Like.' Everyone has to guess."

"That sounds like fun," said Andrew.

"I will go first," I said. I thought a moment about Henry and how old he must be. "I think he is very feeble now," I said. "He has to use a cane. I bet the cane is carved from wood and has a silver elephant on top." I thought that was a very good guess. "Now it is Seth's turn."

"Well," said Seth, "I think Henry has a beard. And I think he wears a pirate's patch over one eye."

I frowned. Seth was not taking my game very seriously.

"Mommy's turn," I said.

"I think he has a big tattoo on one arm," said Mommy. "And I think he has a parrot sitting on one shoulder."

"Mommy," I said. "Please guess for *real*. This is not a joke."

"Okay," she agreed. "I guess that Henry wears wire-rimmed glasses. And I really do think he has a tattoo."

Finally it was Andrew's turn. "I think Henry has a pet salamander," he said. "And the salamander's name is Andrew."

At last we got to Henry's house. When Henry opened the door, I saw that he was nothing like I had guessed. He did not walk with a cane. And he did not have a beard or a pirate's patch, as Seth had guessed. But guess what — Henry did wear wire-rimmed glasses. And Mommy was right — he did have a tattoo!

Henry answered the door wearing a short-sleeved shirt. On his arm was a big tattoo of an anchor. Andrew's mouth dropped open. He pointed to Henry's arm.

"Andrew likes your tattoo," Mommy tried to explain.

"Oh, that old thing," said Henry. He laughed. "I got it when I was in the Navy, long years ago."

Henry invited us into his house. Inside, I saw that Henry was *nothing* like I had imagined. He was not poor. And he was not sick. And he was not all alone in the world. In his living room Henry had photos of the people in his family. There was a photo of his wife, Rose. (Henry said she had died nearly ten

years earlier.) And there were photos of his four children — two boys and two girls. (Henry said that now they were grown men and women.) And finally Henry showed us photos of his six grandchildren.

"Wow," I said. "You have certainly been busy since you left Twelve Forest Drive."

Everyone laughed.

"What about your salamander?" asked Andrew. "Do you have any pictures of him?"

"Salamander?" asked Henry. He looked confused. "I am afraid I do not have a salamander. But I do have some snacks for you. Please sit down. We can have some juice and soda and chips with dip."

When Henry brought the snacks, we all sat down to talk. Henry turned to me.

"After we got off the phone," he said, "I remembered the coins you told me about. In those days I had a small collection, and I wanted to hide them from my little brother, Petey. He was eight and a huge pest. At least, I thought so at the time. So I wrote out the clues and drew the treasure map. Then I put the coins in a box and buried them. Several years later we moved away. I forgot all about the buried coins. In fact, I did not remember anything at all about them until you called."

"Did you know the coins were valuable?" I asked him.

"They were not so valuable at the time. My grandparents had given me a couple of old pennies — "

"One is from the time of the Civil War," I said.

"My goodness!" said Henry. "Was it that old? Most of the coins were probably ones I picked up at the time. Just everyday coins from the nineteen thirties."

"Even those are worth something now," I told him.

Henry shook his head and smiled. "Well, what do you know?" he said.

I had brought the box of coins along. I walked to Henry and placed it in his hands. I cleared my throat importantly.

102

"These coins are yours, Henry," I said. "You buried them many, many years ago. And now they have come back to you. Oh, yes," I said. "I almost forgot."

I pulled out the snapshot of Henry in his short pants.

"Is this you?" I asked. "I found it in the attic."

Henry laughed. "I am afraid that is me," he said. "I guess I have gotten a little older since then."

"And your pants have gotten longer," I said.

Henry opened the lid of the box and picked out one of the old, tarnished coins.

"Karen," he said, "thank you so much. You certainly are a very special young girl."

Henry's Surprise

After I presented the coins to Henry, my family and I drove back to Stoneybrook. A few days later, the doorbell rang. Seth was making a salad for dinner. Mommy was paying bills.

"I'll get it!" I cried. I ran to the window and peered out. "Henry!" I cried. I swung open the door.

"Why, look at this house," he said, peering around. "I have not seen this place since I was a kid."

"Come on in," I said. I took Henry's arm

and pulled him into the living room. Mommy and Seth came out of the kitchen.

"I do not want to interrupt your evening," Henry said. "I just wanted to come by and drop off a little something for Karen."

"For me?" I said.

"Yes. I hope you do not mind that I came by without calling, but I have a present for you."

Behind his back, Henry was holding a box. He pulled it out and handed it to me.

"Cool!" I cried. Mommy threw me a Look. "I mean, thank you very much," I said.

Mommy, Seth, and Andrew gathered around as I tore open the wrapping paper. Inside was a book, *The Basics of Coin Collecting*. Underneath was a clear plastic holder with coins inside. One of the coins was the penny from 1861. It had been cleaned, so it looked new and shiny.

"But, Henry," I protested. "This is *your* coin."

"Not anymore," he said. "I think it should belong to you."

I did not know what to say. (That is very unusual for me.) Now I had the beginning of a coin collection. And I had a book that told me all about coins. But I had even more than that. I had a brand-new hobby.

Mommy and Seth asked Henry to stay for dinner, but he said he had to leave.

"Why don't you come another time?" said Mommy. "We would certainly love to have you."

"I would be honored," said Henry.

"How about this Saturday?" said Mommy.

"That would be perfect," I chimed in. "That is the night of Nancy's ballet recital. After dinner, we could all go see her dance."

"That sounds lovely," said Henry. "An evening of good food and culture."

"Saturday it is," said Mommy.

Henry was about to leave when I remembered something important.

"Before you go," I said, "come with me."

Henry followed me into the dining room.

"Knock on the paneling," I said. "Right here."

Henry rapped on the wood. Out fell the knot. He peered into the hole and pulled out the treasure map. (I had put it back there for safekeeping.) Henry unrolled it and looked at it long and hard, shaking his head.

"You put a lot of thought into burying the coins," I said.

"Well," he replied, "my father always told me, 'A penny saved is a penny earned.'" Henry grinned. "And in this case," he added, "one penny earned quite a bundle, didn't it?"

Nancy's Recital

On Saturday night, Mommy, Seth, Andrew and I made a great dinner. Roast chicken, mashed potatoes, and a big green salad. Yum. The house smelled warm and chickeny. I danced around the kitchen while the chicken popped and sizzled in the oven.

Ding dong!

"Henry's here!" I cried. I ran to the door to let him in.

"My," he said, "don't you look beautiful."

I spun around to show off my dress. It had a lace collar and a pink sash.

"I *have* to look beautiful," I said. "We are going to Nancy's recital."

Seth gave Henry the grand tour of the house. I followed along to help.

"Dinner!" called Mommy.

At the table, it was hard to talk quietly. So much was happening. I was very excited.

"Do not talk with your mouth full," Mommy reminded me.

"Use your indoor voice," said Seth.

Soon it was time to drive to the recital. Henry followed us in his car. Seth bought the tickets at the door. The woman at the cash box gave him some coins as change. I asked Seth if I could see them.

"From now on," I announced, "I will check everyone's coins before they put them in their pockets. Maybe some of the coins are old. Maybe I will need them for my collection."

"Good thinking," said Henry.

Nancy did very well in her recital. I was not sure what her ballet steps were supposed to look like exactly, but they looked very graceful to me. At the end of the dance, she stepped forward with the others to curtsy. She did it just the way I had shown her.

"Yea, Nancy!" I yelled. I clapped so hard my hands hurt.

Up onstage, Nancy ducked her head. She was probably blushing, but I did not care. I was very proud of the work she had done.

After the performance, Nancy came out the stage door and into the audience. I introduced her to Henry.

"I have been very busy while you have been rehearsing," I told Nancy. "I became a detective and found a buried treasure. Henry buried it more than sixty years ago," I said.

"Really?" said Nancy. Her eyes grew round and wide.

Henry complimented Nancy. He told her that she had done a beautiful job onstage. Then he had to leave. He had a long drive back to his house.

We walked Henry to the parking lot.

Nancy and I waved good-bye. Henry was my new friend, and Nancy was my old friend, tried and true.

"You were a great ballerina," I told Nancy. "But I am happy that your recital is over. Now you will be able to play with me again."

"I am happy, too," said Nancy. "Maybe we could play detective."

"We could," I said. "But I have a new hobby now. I am a coin collector."

"Really?" said Nancy.

"Yes," I said. "And I have a *very* valuable collection."

Nancy looked surprised.

"Come on!" I said.

I took her hand and we ran back inside the auditorium. I had so much to tell her.

L. GODWIN

About the Author

Ann M. Martin lives in New York City
and loves animals, especially cats. She has
two cats of her own, Gussie and Woody.

Other books by Ann M. Martin that you
might enjoy are *Stage Fright*; *Me and Katie
(the Pest)*; and the books in *The Baby-sitters
Club* series.

Ann likes ice cream and *I Love Lucy*. And
she has her own little sister, whose name
is Jane.